LIVING THINGS

ROBERT SNEDDEN

Amphibians

A⁺
Smart Apple Media

Published by Smart Apple Media
2140 Howard Drive West
North Mankato, MN 56003

Designed by Guy Callaby
Edited by Pip Morgan
Illustrations by Guy Callaby
Picture research by Su Alexander

Picture acknowledgements
Title page Chris Mattison;Frank Lane Picture Agency/Corbis; 3 Joe McDonald/Corbis;
4 Fabio Liverani/Nature Picture Library; 5t Alan Wight, b Alberto Estrada-Acosta; 6 Robert
Valentic/Nature Picture Library; 7 Morley Read/Nature Picture Library; 8 Kim Taylor/Nature
Picture Library; 9t John Sullivan/Ribbit photography, b Tim MacMillan/John Downer PR/
Nature Picture Library; 11t Fabio Liverani/Nature Picture Library, b Barry Mansell/Nature
Picture Library; 12 Chris Mattison;Frank Lane Picture Agency/Corbis; 13 Peter Oxford/
Nature Picture Library; 14 Michael & Patricia Fogden/Corbis; 15t Jim Zuckerman/Corbis,
b Joe McDonald/Corbis; 16 Professor Jack Dermid/Oxford Scientific Films; 17t Tom
Brakefield/Corbis, b Henk Wallays; 18 Kathie Atkinson/Oxford Scientific Films; 19t Stephen
Deban, b Paulo de Oliveira/Oxford Scientific Films; 20 Tim Martin/Nature Picture Library;
21t Joyce Gross, b Henk Wallays; 22 Christoph Bork; 23 John Cancalosi/Nature Picture
Library; 24 Michael Fogden/Oxford Scientific Films; 25t Kim Taylor/Nature Picture Library,
b Henk Wallays; 27 Jane Burton/Nature Picture Library; 28 Albert S Feng; 29 Ken Griffiths/
NHPA

Front cover: Tom Brakefield/Corbis

Printed in China

Library of Congress Cataloging-in-Publication Data

Snedden, Robert.
Amphibians / by Robert Snedden.
p. cm. — (Living things)
Includes index.
ISBN-13: 978-1-59920-075-0
1. Amphibians—Juvenile literature. I. Title.

QL644.2.S674 2007
597'.6—dc22   2006036877

First Edition

9 8 7 6 5 4 3 2 1

Contents

What is an amphibian?

You probably know what frogs and toads are. Perhaps you've heard of newts, too. But what about salamanders or caecilians (pronounced sey-SILL-yins)? All these animals are amphibians.

One of the things that makes amphibians different from other animals is that they spend at least part of their lives in water and part on land. In this book, we will look at the many ways in which amphibians are suited to this double life.

Amphibians are among the most fascinating and colorful of the earth's inhabitants. This red-eyed tree frog from South America would probably stand out on any planet!

Changing shapes

Have you ever kept tadpoles in a tank or seen them in a pond? If you have, you might have watched them change shape as they became adults. Slowly, the wriggling, legless tadpoles lose their tails, grow legs, and become swimming, jumping frogs. This is one of the most fascinating things about amphibians—many of them change from one shape into another during their life cycle. In fact, young and adult amphibians often have completely different lifestyles.

BELOW *The California tiger salamander is one of many amphibians that are in danger of extinction because their habitats are disappearing.*

Shapes and sizes

Amphibians come in a variety of shapes and sizes. There are tiny frogs that could sit on a person's fingernail and giant salamanders nearly six and a half feet (2 m) long. Some amphibians are very brightly colored, while others blend in so well with their surroundings they are difficult to see.

Amphibians live all over the world. Some spend all their lives on land and some live in water, but all need some sort of moisture to survive. So let's find out just what an amphibian is.

This tiny frog from the forests of Cuba is the smallest four-legged animal in the world.

WOW!

The world's smallest amphibian is a Cuban frog. When fully grown, it is 0.3 to 0.4 inches (8.5–12 mm) long. It is also the smallest four-legged animal. The biggest amphibian ever was a Chinese giant salamander that measured 5.9 feet (1.8 m) from the snout to the tip of the tail.

Legs and tails . . . or not!

All amphibians can be grouped into three basic types—
those with legs and tails, those with legs but no tails, and
those with tails but no legs!

BELOW *The Asian black-spined toad is a good example of how toads have rougher skin than smooth-skinned frogs.*

LEFT *This caecilian is especially colorful and lives throughout the South American rain forests.*

Salamanders and newts

Salamanders look a little like lizards and are sometimes mistaken for them. But salamanders are amphibians—and lizards are reptiles. There are all types of salamanders. Some salamanders spend all their lives in water and some only go into water to breed. Others spend almost their entire lives on land, though they are never far from water. Newts are small salamanders that live in the water.

Frogs and toads

Frogs and toads live almost anywhere there is fresh water. They usually have long back legs, short bodies, and big heads with large mouths. What's the difference between a frog and a toad? Actually, all toads are a type of frog, but toads have rougher skin than other frogs and a lot of warts. Toads live mostly on land, and other frogs live on land and in water. Toads usually have shorter back legs for walking or taking short hops, rather than leaping like other frogs.

Caecilians

Caecilians are rare creatures that look different from other amphibians. They do not have legs and look a little like large earthworms. Caecilians live in tropical places. Most are burrowers—they use their hard, shovel-like heads to push their way through the damp soil. Some live in streams and spend all their lives in the water. Caecilians range in size from four inches (10 cm) to more than three feet (0.9 m) long.

WOW!

Rain forests are home to the greatest variety of frogs. Scientists have found 80 different kinds in a 1.2-square-mile (3 sq km) area of forest in Ecuador. Europe only has about 30 different types of amphibians.

Getting around

Amphibians travel from place to place in a variety of ways. Frogs jump, toads hop, salamanders walk or run, while caecilians simply wriggle like worms through the soil.

A frog's back legs can be very powerful. Its strong thigh muscles straighten the back legs, pushing its feet hard against the ground and propelling the frog forward, out of danger. The front legs act like shock absorbers when the frog lands. Toads don't jump. They hop or walk along the ground.

BELOW *A frog launches itself into the air with a sudden, strong push of its long, powerful back legs. The average frog can leap at least ten times its own body length.*

Flippers for swimming
The skin between the toes of frogs and toads is called webbing and is very useful for swimming. The webbed feet on the back legs push against the water like a diver's flippers and they propel the animal forward, while the front legs are used for steering.

Salamander stroll

Salamanders have four legs that are usually all the same size. They don't jump—they walk or run, sometimes along the bottom of the pond where they live. Salamanders are good swimmers, too. They use their strong tails to propel themselves through the water. Some salamanders spend most of their lives in the water and have very weak legs.

LEFT *Unlike frogs, salamanders can't jump. They walk steadily along, putting one front foot and the opposite back foot forward at the same time.*

Flying frog

Some tree frogs use their webbed feet to glide through the air. They stretch out the webbing between their fingers and toes as they leap from branch to branch. The webbing acts like a parachute and helps the frog stay in the air longer. Some can travel more than 130 feet (40 m) through the air. Sticky pads on their feet help them grab a tree branch and land safely.

WOW!

The Mount Lyell salamander lives under rocks. If it is disturbed, it will curl into a ball and roll down a hillside to escape from danger.

Legless diggers

Caecilians have no legs at all. They use their powerful heads to dig into the soft, damp soil of their tropical homes. They have strong, flexible bodies and wriggle like worms through their burrows.

RIGHT *The big webbed feet of this tree frog help it glide from branch to branch. This is a good way to find a meal or to escape being eaten.*

Breathing in and out of water

All animals need oxygen to survive. It helps them get energy from the food they eat. Most large land animals breathe oxygen into their lungs. Amphibians use their lungs, too, but this is not the only way they can get the oxygen they need.

Frog breathing

The lungs of an amphibian are like very thin bags and are much more simple than the lungs of mammals, such as humans.

A frog doesn't breathe by expanding its chest, as we do. Its throat moves down and draws in air through its nostrils. As the nostrils close, the throat moves up and this movement forces air into the frog's lungs. To breathe out, the frog's throat moves down again, drawing air out of the lungs. Finally, the nostrils open again and the throat moves up, pushing the air out.

FROG HEART AND LUNGS

arteries (carry oxygen-rich blood)

veins (carry blood without much oxygen)

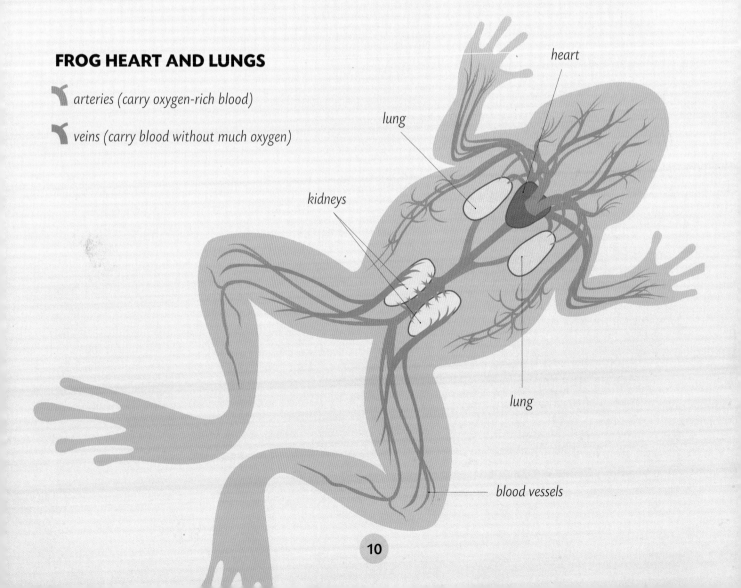

heart

lung

kidneys

lung

blood vessels

Breathe, skin!

An amphibian's skin is unlike that of any other animal. It is very thin and smooth and is covered with a slimy substance called mucus, so it feels moist to the touch. Amphibians have many blood vessels just beneath the surface of the skin. Oxygen dissolves in the mucus and then passes into the blood vessels. The wonderful thing about using skin for breathing is that it works as well under water it does on land.

Amphibians can also breathe through the moist lining of their mouths. Oxygen dissolves in the lining and passes into the blood vessels of the mouth. Some salamanders do not have lungs, and they get all the oxygen they need through their mouths and skin.

Gills

Most young amphibians spend all their time in water. They do not have lungs, but instead breathe using feathery gills. The gills are packed with tiny blood vessels that absorb the oxygen that is dissolved in the water. Usually, amphibians lose their gills when they become adults. Some, such as the mud puppy (a type of salamander), keep their gills into adulthood.

ABOVE *This crested newt larva has gills, which you can see protruding from the back of its head. They allow the larva to breathe under water.*

LEFT *The northern dusky salamander, which lives in the United States, does not have lungs, so it breathes through its skin.*

Not too hot and not too cold

A cold amphibian moves very slowly. Unlike birds and mammals, amphibians are cold-blooded—the energy they get from their food does not keep them warm.

Amphibians warm themselves from the outside when they are cold. Usually this means sitting in the sun until they reach the right temperature. Once they are warm enough, they are ready to begin the day's amphibian activities. If they get too hot, they find some shade and cool off again.

LEFT *The Australian water-holding frog can store water in its bladder for months at a time.*

WOW!

The Australian water-holding frog can wait up to seven years for rain to fall in the desert where it lives. This frog burrows underground and protects itself from drying out in a cocoon made of skin that it has shed.

Hibernation

Amphibians hibernate if they live in countries where the climate is cold in winter. As winter approaches and the temperature drops, amphibians find places to protect themselves from the cold. For example, they will burrow into the mud on the bottom of a pond or hide beneath a pile of leaves. As the amphibian's heart starts to beat more slowly, its body temperature falls, and it enters the deep, sleep-like state of hibernation.

Water cooling

An amphibian's moist skin is good for breathing in and out of water, but it does not help the animal stay warm. On hot days, or when exercising, humans cool off by sweating. As the water from the sweat evaporates into the air, it takes away the heat energy from our bodies. Amphibians have permanently moist skin, so they are in danger of being cold all the time. They are also at risk of drying out. This is one reason most amphibians live in damp places.

ABOVE *Many rain forest salamanders are nocturnal, avoiding the heat of the day and hunting at night when it is cooler.*

WOW!

The wood frog can survive very cold conditions. More than half the water in its body can turn to ice—and it will still thaw and revive when spring comes. The frog's vital organs, such as its heart and lungs, are protected by a natural antifreeze, which keeps them from freezing.

Seeing and hearing

Burrowing caecilians spend most of their time underground, and they are practically blind. Their eyes are covered by skin and sometimes bone. However, sight is a very important sense for other amphibians.

Don't move!

Salamanders and frogs have very good eyesight. A frog's big eyes help it see almost all the way around its body without moving its head. A frog can see even the slightest movement. A tasty flying insect moving across a frog's line of sight is soon snapped up. But frogs have a hard time seeing things that don't move. An insect that stays still won't be spotted, no matter how hungry the frog is.

WOW!

The Panamanian golden frog doesn't have any ears, but it still makes calls and responds to sounds. Biologists think that the frog's lungs, which are just under its skin, act as a substitute for ears.

Up periscope!

If you look carefully at the surface of a pond where frogs live, you might see a pair of large eyes poking up above the surface like a submarine's periscope. Having eyes on the tops of their heads is also helpful to frogs on land. Tree frogs have good all-around vision, which helps them spot predators, such as birds. Many frogs are active at night and have very good night vision.

Frogs and toads can't see very well under water because a thin, skin-like membrane covers each eye to protect it. This membrane isn't completely transparent, so the frog can't see as well through it.

Can frogs see in color? Many types of frogs are very colorful, particularly during the mating season, so chances are they can. There isn't much point in trying to attract a color-blind mate by being brightly colored!

ABOVE *You can clearly see this frog's eardrum just behind its eye.*

This bullfrog stays well hidden in the duckweed, and only its watchful eyes are visible.

Listen to this!

Amphibians have good hearing, although probably not as good as ours. Frogs and toads have the best hearing of all the amphibians. They don't have external ears that hear sound, but if you look carefully, you can see little circles just behind a frog's eyes, which are its eardrums. The eardrums are like tightly stretched, thin layers of skin that pick up sound vibrations traveling through air and water.

Talking to each other is important for frogs and toads. They can make a wide variety of calls with their voice box, or larynx, and a large expanding vocal sac that is attached to the throat. Some calls attract mates, some scare off rivals, and other calls warn of danger.

Tastes, smells, and vibrations

Amphibians can taste and smell, and some are able to sense vibrations in the water. Taste and smell are called chemical senses because they detect a chemical or combination of chemicals in water, air, or food.

Does it taste bad?

Amphibians and mammals have tongues with taste buds, but birds, fish, and reptiles do not. A sense of taste is important because it can warn an animal that something is bad to eat. For example, some insects have a nasty taste, which protects them from being eaten by hungry amphibians. If amphibians catch one of these insects, they quickly spit them out again.

BELOW *The mud puppy is a North American salamander that spends its whole life in water and is very sensitive to the presence of different odors.*

Detecting smells

Smells are carried through the air. You detect a smell when the chemical that is the source of the smell dissolves in the moist lining of your nose. Amphibians have chemical detectors all over their moist bodies, as well as inside their nostrils and mouths. This makes amphibians very sensitive to chemical pollution.

The sense of smell is important to amphibians. Newts, for example, often find their food by smelling it. When they find something to eat, they get excited and they may attack other newts that get too close to their prize. When they come out of hibernation in the spring, newts use their sense of smell to find their way back to the water.

ABOVE *The African clawed frog has a well-developed lateral line that allows it to detect movements in the water.*

Good vibrations

Amphibians that spend all their time in water are sensitive to vibrations that travel through the water. Such amphibians include most tadpoles and some adults, such as the clawed frog and the hellbender (a type of salamander). Like fish, they have a line of vibration detectors in their skin called a lateral line. These detectors are sensitive to changes in the flow of water and let the amphibian know when something is moving through the water nearby. This sense helps amphibians find their way around the bottom of murky ponds.

Feeling the way

A caecilian has sensitive tentacles on either side of its head, between its nostrils and its eyes. The tentacles help the caecilian feel its way along its burrow, and find its prey. The tentacles are also sensitive to chemicals, which allows the caecilian to "taste" its way around. When they are not in use, the tentacles are safely stored in grooves along the caecilian's head.

ABOVE *You can see the sensitive tentacles of this caecilian just below its eye, at the front of its head.*

WOW!

Amphibians can smell danger. A salamander can detect a hungry trout nearby and will hide to avoid it. Female salamanders will even avoid laying their eggs in ponds where they can smell fish nearby.

Meal time

Amphibians are not fussy eaters. Many of them will eat just about anything they can catch and fit into their mouths. Only the size of its head puts a limit on what a frog will eat.

Most amphibians are meat-eaters. Bigger frogs and toads enjoy a wide menu of fish, reptiles, birds, and small mammals. They readily eat insects, snails, and the tadpoles of other amphibians. They may even eat smaller adult amphibians as well.

Salamanders and newts eat pond-dwelling insects, worms, slugs, and other inhabitants of damp places. Amphibians care so little about what they eat that young tadpoles from the same batch of eggs will eat each other if there isn't anything else available.

BELOW *A large toad eats a frog, which shows that amphibians will eat anything they can, even each other.*

Some salamanders can flick out their long tongues at an extraordinary speed to catch insects.

It's on the tip of my tongue . . .

Frogs and salamanders catch their food using their extra special tongues. A frog's tongue lies folded in its mouth ready to strike at anything that looks interesting. Unlike your tongue, which is attached at the back of your mouth, a frog's tongue is attached at the front of its mouth. A sticky tip on the frog tongue makes sure the food is caught. Some salamanders from the tropics can shoot out their tongues up to four-fifths the length of their bodies. They do this in just a fraction of a second.

Chewing eyeballs

A frog's eyes don't just help it catch a meal. They help the frog swallow it, too. Many frogs have teeth, but they are too small and weak to be used for chewing. Instead, the frog pulls its eyeballs down into its head, while at the same time it presses its tongue up, so the prey is squashed between the tongue and eyeballs and pushed down the frog's throat. Imagine watching that from across the dinner table!

RIGHT *A toad pulls its eyeballs into its head to help this tasty centipede on its way down the throat.*

WOW!

Most amphibians never take a drink of water because they can absorb all the water they need through their skin.

WOW!

If a frog eats something it doesn't like, it can pop its stomach out of its mouth and wipe it clean with its front legs!

A bite to eat

A caecilian's mouth is full of needle-like teeth to help it grab hold of its prey. Caecilians eat various creatures, such as small lizards or snakes, beetles or termites, or other amphibians, such as frogs or even fellow caecilians. Like other amphibians, caecilians don't chew their food, but swallow it whole or in bite-sized chunks.

Staying alive

Just as amphibians like to eat many things, many things like to eat amphibians. Luckily for the amphibians, they have a few defense strategies to use. Sometimes, if you're a frog, this can be as simple as using your powerful legs to leap away from the danger. There are also other things an amphibian can do.

Danger, poison!

The moist mucus that covers an amphibian's skin may be poisonous —sometimes very poisonous. Newts and poison arrow frogs are particularly harmful to any animal that tries to eat one. If they are attacked, some amphibians can spray poison into the air through tiny openings in their bodies. Poisonous amphibians are generally brightly colored, a clear warning to predators that they are not good to eat.

BELOW *The bright colors of a strawberry poison arrow frog make it stand out and they act as a warning to predators that it is definitely not good to eat.*

Where did it go?

It's not good to be bitten by a predator, even if the predator gets an upset stomach. A good way to avoid being attacked is to stay hidden. Many salamanders stay very still when faced with a predator, flattening themselves so they are more difficult to spot. To help them hide, they have colors that camouflage them, so they blend into their surroundings.

Many frogs are also difficult to spot. Tree frogs are often green, a hard color to see against a background of leaves! Others may blend in with the bark of the trees they live on. Some frogs pretend to be something else. If a predator comes near, they show a pattern on their body that looks just like the eyes of an owl or a snake. This can startle an attacker and allow the frog to escape.

ABOVE *This gray tree frog is well camouflaged against the bark of the tree where it makes its home.*

RIGHT *A salamander has lost its tail, but is starting to grow another one.*

WOW!

The poison produced by many of the poison frogs of South and Central America (called batrachotoxin), is so powerful that just 0.00001 grams is enough to kill an adult human.

The end of the tail

Some salamanders trick their prey. They lash their tails back and forth, drawing the attention of the predator. There are two reasons for this: First, the tail can take a lot of damage before the salamander is seriously harmed. In fact, some salamanders can lose their tails altogether and simply grow a new one. Second, the tail is loaded with poison, an unwelcome surprise for the attacker.

A new generation

Like almost all animals, adult amphibians seek mates so they can produce young. The eggs produced by a female are fertilized by a male and then grow into young amphibians.

Finding a mate

Many amphibians, especially frogs and toads, return to the pond or stream where they were born to find a mate. This journey often means they have to travel long distances.

An amphibian meeting place can be noisy. Large numbers of males are usually the first to arive on the scene. At first, everything is quiet, but after a few days, the amphibians begin to call loudly to each other. This calling is actually a battle for territory.

BELOW *During the breeding season the male banded newt develops a spectacular crest along its back and tail, and its colors become brighter.*

After a while, the female amphibians begin to arrive. Then the males change their call from "Keep away!" to "Over here! Over here!" as they try to attract the females' attention. The strongest frogs generally have the loudest calls and they will most likely find a mate.

Salamanders and newts find their mates much more quietly. The male newt tries to attract a female by doing a mating dance that shows off his colorful markings and by waving a special scent toward her with his tail. The waving tail makes waves in the water, making him difficult to ignore.

At the moment, no one is quite sure how caecilians find a mate in their burrows, although scent helps the process.

LEFT *A male common frog clings to a female's back to fertilize her eggs as she lays them. The mass of eggs is called spawn.*

Laying eggs

When a female frog is ready to lay her eggs, her mate climbs on her back. As she produces the eggs, the male releases a milky fluid over the eggs to fertilize them.

Salamander eggs are fertilized before the female lays them. The male salamander produces a tiny, jelly-like package that the female takes in through a special opening in her body. Inside the female's body, the jelly dissolves and her eggs are fertilized and ready to be laid.

Many caecilians don't lay eggs. The male can fertilize the female's eggs inside her body, and the female gives birth to live young. Some salamanders also produce live young.

Eggs and tadpoles

Unlike the eggs of reptiles and birds, amphibian eggs do not have a shell to protect them. They have to be laid in water to prevent them from drying out. This is why frogs and toads return to ponds and streams to breed.

Looking after the eggs

Most amphibians lay their eggs and then forget about them. Fish and other animals eat many of the abandoned eggs before they can develop. However, some amphibians take care of their eggs. For example, the male midwife toad carries his eggs wrapped around his waist. He is careful to make sure the eggs don't dry out. When they are ready to hatch, he returns to a pond, backing into it so that the tadpoles can hatch in the water.

When the eggs of the Darwin's frog hatch, the male gathers the tadpoles in his throat pouch where they stay until they become adults. One type of Australian frog does more than that: the female swallows her eggs and they develop into tadpoles in her stomach.

BELOW *A male Darwin's frog from South America sits with the tiny young frogs he has kept safe in his throat pouch.*

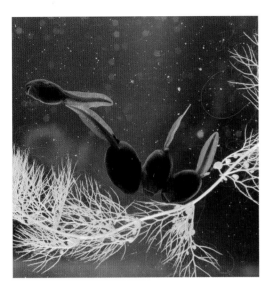

ABOVE *If they survive long enough, these tadpoles will eventually grow into adult common toads.*

Larvae life

When it is inside the egg, the young amphibian is called an embryo; when it emerges, it is called a larva. With their legless bodies and long tails, the larvae don't look anything like the adults. For the first few days of their lives, the larvae remain attached to the yolk from the egg and this supplies them with food.

Salamander larvae are hunters like their parents. They catch and eat water fleas and other small creatures, including salamander larvae smaller than they are. The larvae of frogs and toads, usually called tadpoles, graze on pond plants at first, but as they grow older they turn their attention to other water-dwellers.

Life is dangerous for a young amphibian that has just hatched from its egg. Water beetles, dragonfly larvae, fish, birds, and adult amphibians are among the many animals that like a tasty tadpole. As the surviving young grow older, their bodies change as they gradually become adult amphibians.

RIGHT *Young caecilians wind around each other in a wriggling ball.*

WOW!

The female marsupial frog has a pouch, just like a kangaroo, where she keeps her eggs. When the eggs hatch into tadpoles, she opens the pouch with her toes and lets them out into the water.

Reaching adulthood

Amphibians, like many insects, have larvae that look very different from the adults. The change from larva to adult is called metamorphosis. Caecilians, however, do not change. The only difference between a young caecilian and an adult is that the young have gills and the adults have lungs.

LIFE CYCLE OF THE FROG

A frog begins life as an embryo in an egg. This hatches into a tadpole, which changes into an adult.

Metamorphosis

Insect larvae go through a quiet resting stage while they change into adults, but amphibians stay active while they change. One of the first signs that a tadpole is beginning the change to adulthood is when it starts coming to the surface to take little gulps of air. Tadpoles breathe by using their gills to take oxygen from the water. The trips to the surface mean that the tadpole's lungs are starting to develop. When the tadpole is fully adult, it will use its lungs to breathe on land.

Best foot forward

Next, the young amphibian begins to grow legs. The front legs are the first to appear in salamanders. In frogs, the back legs come first. At the same time the young frog is also losing its tail. The tail doesn't just fall off. It is absorbed into the tadpole's body as a useful source of food. Salamanders keep their tails into adulthood.

Gradually, the tadpole's shape changes until it looks like an adult. All four legs are in position and its eyes have grown bigger. Now it is ready to leave the water and explore life on land. Metamorphosis only takes about six days for the tadpoles of desert frogs, which hatch in rapidly disappearing rain puddles. Some salamanders stretch the process out over six months.

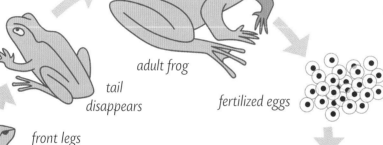

adult frog

tail disappears

fertilized eggs

front legs develop

embryos develop

hind legs develop

legless tadpoles

larvae hatch

WOW!

The giant salamander is not only the biggest amphibian in the world, it is also the one that lives the longest—they have been known to live for 55 years.

LEFT *The rare Mexican axolotl is the "Peter Pan" of the amphibians— it never grows up. It keeps its gills all through its life and is almost like a big, four-legged tadpole.*

Forever young

Some salamanders, such as the axolotl, never completely grow up. Even when they are fully grown, they still keep some of the features they had as tadpoles. For instance, they have gills throughout their lives and lack the big eyes of other adult salamanders.

WOW!

American greenhouse frogs don't lay their eggs in water but in damp places on land. The tadpole stage of the animal's life takes place in the egg, and a tiny version of an adult frog emerges after about two weeks.

Amphibian planet

Amphibians are special creatures. Their life cycles bridge the two worlds of water and land. The name amphibian means "both lives"—a life on land and a life in water.

Amphibians begin as soft, vulnerable eggs, then hatch into larvae, living in the water as they slowly grow into adults. As air-breathing adults, they are at home on the land, but they never stray too far from water.

Millions of years ago, amphibians were among the first animals to leave the sea and live at least partly on the land. They were the "pioneers." Now amphibians live all over the world, from high mountain meadows to tropical forests. All they need is moisture and temperatures that are not too cold in the winter.

ABOVE *Concave-eared torrent frogs from China are rare amphibians that produce high-pitched sounds so they can hear themselves above the noise of the waterfalls where they live.*

Amphibian variety

Amphibians have developed many ways to survive on this planet. For example, there are toads that give birth to live young instead of laying eggs. There are salamanders that spend their entire lives in water, never coming out on dry land.

Early warnings

One thing all amphibians have in common is their delicate, moist skin. Amphibian skin is very useful because it allows oxygen and water to pass through. The problem is that this wonderful skin doesn't give the amphibian much protection from water or air pollution. Because amphibians are so sensitive to pollution, a drop in their numbers can be an early warning signal that all is not well in the environment.

There are fewer than 6,000 different kinds of amphibians in the world. The numbers of nearly half of these are falling, and around one-third are threatened with extinction. In the last 20 years or so, more than 100 kinds of amphibians have disappeared and they may be gone forever. These changes in the amphibian populations are a signal that it's time to clean up the planet.

LEFT *The corroboree frog is one of the world's rarest amphibians. It lives within a small 154-square-mile (400 sq km) area of New South Wales in Australia.*

Glossary

Blood vessels Networks of tubes that carry blood around the body. Veins carry blood to the lungs to pick up oxygen, and arteries carry the oxygen to the body.

Camouflage Colors or patterns on an amphibian or other animal that make it hard to see against its surroundings.

Cold-blooded Describes an animal that can't generate warmth from the food it eats; amphibians, fish, and reptiles are all cold-blooded.

Extinction What happens when all the members of a particular type of plant or animal have died out and no more exist anywhere.

Fertilize To make an egg fertile; a male amphibian fertilizes the female's eggs so they can develop into young amphibians.

Gills Parts of the body young amphibians use to get oxygen from water; gills do what lungs do for air-breathing animals.

Habitat The place where a living thing makes its home.

Hibernation A sleep-like state that some animals enter as a way of surviving harsh winter conditions. During hibernation, the animal's temperature falls and its heart and other organs work more slowly.

Larva (plural: larvae) The young of an amphibian after it hatches from the egg. The larva does not look like the adult animal it will become. The change from larva to adult is called metamorphosis. Young insects are also called larvae.

Larynx The vocal cords, or voice box; air passing through the larynx makes it vibrate to produce sounds.

Lateral line A system of detectors along the side of some amphibians that can detect movements and vibrations in the water; fish also have lateral line detectors.

Lungs Parts of the body that larger animals, such as amphibians, mammals, and birds, use to get oxygen from the air.

Mate One of a pair of animals, one male and the other female, that produce young together; doing this is called mating.

Mating season   The time of year when the males and females of a type of animal find each other to produce young.

Membrane   A thin, skin-like covering.

Metamorphosis   The process of change from a larva to an adult amphibian.

Mucus   A slightly sticky fluid that an amphibian produces to protect its skin.

Spawn   The eggs of an amphibian.

Tadpole   The larva of a frog or toad.

Taste buds   Tiny taste detectors usually found on the upper surface of the tongue.

Tentacles   Fleshy feelers that some animals use to find their way around or hunt for food.

Territory   The area an amphibian or other animal lives in, which it defends from others; many frogs call to announce to others where their territory is.

Webbing   Thin skin connecting an amphibian's toes and fingers.

Web sites

http://cgee.hamline.edu/frogs
A Web site from the Center for Global Environmental Education that explores the world of frogs.

**www.sandiegozoo.org/animalbytes/
t-caecilian.html**
Caecilian facts and pictures from the San Diego Zoo.

www.exploratorium.edu/frogs/
Information on "The Amazing Adaptable Frog."

**http://animaldiversity.ummz.umich.edu/site/
topics/frogCalls.html**
MP3 files of a variety of frog calls. Hear them for yourself.

http://nationalzoo.si.edu/Publications/ZooGoer/2000/2/waterdogsmudpuppieshellbender.cfm
"On Waterdogs, Mudpuppies, and the Occasional Hellbender." An informative article on salamanders from the Smithsonian ZooGoer. There are lots of articles about other amphibians, too!

Index